# lovely seeds

a walk through the garden of our becoming

## R.H. SWANEY

central avenue publishing

2018

Published by Central Avenue Publishing, an imprint of Central Avenue Marketing Ltd.
www.centralavenuepublishing.com

**LOVELY SEEDS**

Trade Paperback: 978-1-77168-148-3
Epub: 978-1-77168-149-0
Mobi: 978-1-77168-150-6


Published in Canada
Printed in United States of America

1. POETRY / General    2. POETRY / Inspirational

10 9 8 7 6 5 4 3 2 1

## SEED

The peaceful places in our heads we yearn to exist in
are where we find the seeds of our becoming.

## SOIL

We must find the most fertile soil and lose ourselves in
all the nourishment it has to offer.

## WATER

We hold a handful of seeds that we can only water by
letting our well spill over.

## GROWTH

As our stems sprout, we can offer what we've learned
about what it means to grow to the ones around us.

## BLOOM

When our petals begin to show, our valiant colors give
hope to those who need it most.

## RESTORE

Our leaves wilt and fall to the ground.

# *SEED*

The peaceful places in our heads we yearn to exist in are where we find the seeds of our becoming.

## WEATHER TALK

I wish we could talk about our hearts like we talk about the weather, because whether or not we are okay is more important than the chance of rain.

The condition of our brains is more important than the amount of snow, more important than the direction the wind blows.

Imagine, for a minute, a severe-weather warning system for the storms in our heads. It tells us when clouds are forming above each other, allowing us to be there at the first flash of lightning and crack of thunder.

## APPOINTMENTS

There is no shame in seeing a therapist to empty the contents
of your brain to analyze the pieces more closely.

*Keep* the appointments.

*Keep* pursuing the sanity you deserve.

## THE VOICES IN OUR HEADS

I see you whisper to yourself.

I watch you softly move your mouth when no one else is
around as if you are singing a psalm.

You walk the same road every single day to the same bench
where you pass the time.

Some days when I see you walking
and hear you loudly talking,
I'd like to believe that you are scolding the demons that
haunt your delicate mind.

Other days I feel a peace resonate from your bones.

I know there are wars waging in your head,
but your outer self maintains a sense of calm.

Don't we all talk to ourselves?
Yet, we choose to keep it inside.

We all have those wars,
just some of us deal with them differently.

What matters most is that we all keep breathing,
for our breath is the outcome of our will to keep living.

Isn't there victory here? *I believe there is.*

## WAITING FOR THE STORM TO PASS, TOGETHER

If you want to curl up in a ball and lie on the kitchen floor,
I'll curl up next to you 'til you don't feel that way anymore.

Don't apologize for being sad.

You can't help what happens inside your own head.

If you want to spend the day just lying in bed, I'll lie next to
you 'til you're happy again.

## FEEBLE ADVICE FROM WELL-INTENTIONED FRIENDS

You cannot run from what is haunting you
if what plagues you comes from within.

It hurts when they tell you to *just relax*,
because you know your brain doesn't work that way.

You wouldn't tell the tree to be like the flower,
or the flower to be like the tree.

So why do they think it's that easy?

—*I apologize for the ones who have minimized your pain.*

## WHAT WE SEE BEFORE WE SLEEP

We find serenity in our rooms away from the noise of the news and social events that give us anxiety.

We are able to get away from everything, everything except ourselves.

I am reminded of this as I lie in bed at night, haunted by the cracks in the ceiling as they slither like serpents towards my head.

## BROKEN GLASS

You knocked the vase off the counter just to watch
something so beautiful shatter into a thousand pieces.

You could relate, because it happened to you.

## A POST-IT NOTE ON MY DESK

Your mental illness is not a burden.

Your anxiety is not an inconvenience.

Never forget, we're all in this together.

## THE QUIET BEFORE THE THUNDER

There is a moment between the freeing feeling of easy breathing and the overwhelming weight that settles on your chest when the anxiety hits.

I call this *"the calm before the storm,"*

a reminder of what it'll feel like when the clouds clear.

## THE BROKEN RECORD OF FRIENDS WHO DON'T UNDERSTAND

When we are hurting, don't let anyone tell us
we need to get over it.

They need to get over the idea that someone else's pain is an
inconvenience to them.

Telling someone to get over it is like telling the stars not to
shine, the moon not to come out at night, or the sun not to
share its warmth.

It's just not possible to flip a switch that does not exist.

We'll move on when we're ready, not when you are tired of
listening to our struggles.

## *REVITALIZE*

When we are broken, we don't just tear ourselves down
completely and start over. We leave the beautiful pieces
as the foundation and revitalize around them.
The structure of who we are remains. We just mend the
holes and reinforce the walls. We add paint and give
ourselves a new purpose. We don't erase our history,
rather, we use it to learn and grow.

## RAIN PUDDLE

The distorted reflection of my face in the rain puddle I just stepped in is a reminder of what I see when I look in the mirror those mornings I don't quite feel myself.

I must remember,
the ripple will always dissipate into clarity.

## BREATH

Take a moment to realize that your breath is the very difference between life and death.

So inhale, exhale, and be in awe of how you save yourself every time you breathe in.

## BAREFOOT AND CAREFREE

The current pulls us in any direction it pleases.

We grow scared as the waves approach ferociously.

But as they find their way to the shore, they peacefully wash the feet of those who walk barefoot on the beach.

It's as if they understand the fragility of our souls.

There is *hope* to be found here.

## MY BROKEN PARTS

I was a sidewalk full of broken cement, overgrown with weeds, and dimly lit at night.

You were the soul brave enough to travel my brokenness.

## GOOD MORNING

Sometimes, the bravest thing you'll do in a day is get out of bed, and that is still worth *rejoicing* over.

## A DAY IN MY HEAD IS A DAY IN CHAOS

I tried to make a list of every moment I had it all together, but the page was just as empty as the free time I don't have because my planner is full of monotonous activities I will probably never get to.

Yet, *it is okay* to be this beautiful mess that I am.

## THE DAYS WE FEEL MOST ALONE

Every breath that spills from your lungs is a gift to yourself and the ones that you love.

You add value to this world.

My plea to you: *never give up.*

When you are drowning in pain, struggling to stay afloat, there are hands extended towards you from people who love you more than you know.

Never stop reaching.

You'll either pull yourself up, or get pulled up.

Either is *triumph.*

## EVERY BREATH IS A VICTORY

Even when the hurt keeps you in bed, remember your breath
and the victory in the rise and fall of your chest.

## FREEDOM

There is an ocean in my chest. My lungs rise and fall, as waves crash around my heart. And guess what: I never learned how to swim.

You might see me as a nearly invisible passerby, the person who sits quietly at your favorite coffee shop and keeps to himself.

Most mistake my quiet demeanor, *always-nice-to-others* outer shell, for someone who has it together.

You might see some sense of peace, but I am in danger of drowning.

At an early age, I learned to doggy paddle to stay afloat.

I was told,

*"Keep it inside, kid, no one else can know about the things you think about that keep you up at night."*

At an early age, I learned that talking about my feelings was a sign of weakness.

I learned that boys aren't supposed to cry. So I kept the tears inside until they became an ocean.

And for the past ten years, I've barely been afloat.

I desperately reach for every piece of driftwood I can find.

I eventually realized that there's got to be something more
than this life of drowning.

I began to let myself *feel*.

Slowly, the years of being told talking about my feelings was
not okay spill out of my chest.

Every tear, the water lowers.

And as the fear of speaking out about the thoughts
in my head leaves me, so does this ocean that
has kept me under.

The water spills out, my feet touch the bottom, and for the
first time in my life, I am free of the stigma of mental illness.

# *SOIL*

We must find the most fertile soil and lose ourselves in all
the nourishment it has to offer.

## IF WE WERE TREES

Let the shame you feel about your brain being ill fall from your limbs like the leaves fall from the trees.

Let your branches be free from the weight of self-hate.

The only way to grow is to shed yourself of the old.

*Spring always comes.*

## FLIPPING THROUGH PHOTOS WITH GRANDMA

I remember going through newly developed photographs with my grandma.

We'd find humor in the ones where my
grandpa's finger would disrupt the composition,
most of which would get tossed.

I wish our thoughts were more like these photographs.

The ones that we like most end up in frames upon our mantels, and the ones that give us pain get thrown away and forgotten forever.

## THE MUSIC OF OUR DANCING RIBS

You are worthy of the breath you just took.

So take in another, and another, and another, until your lungs are filled and your ribs dance to the music of existence.

## PRAISE SONGS

The deafening voice in your head proclaiming you aren't good enough can be drowned out by a chorus of everything beautiful and wonderful and extraordinary about you.

I will forever sing,

*"You are infinitely lovely."*

## WHAT WE WEREN'T TAUGHT AS KIDS

It's okay to cry. Every tear is a river gracefully flowing
through the pain, taking your heart to a place
it can finally rest.

## DIRT

Sometimes I feel unwanted,
like the mud beneath one's shoe.

When in reality, I am like the soil
where beautiful flowers bloom.

## BREAKING THE CURSE

You carry the pain from your childhood like an old habit
you just can't shake.

But you aren't defined by what your parents did.

So take a moment to close your eyes and let the weight
from your family of origin waterfall to the ground
and wash your tired feet.

I pray you find peace and become free.

## THE HANDS OF A CLOCK

Time is a road that runs between the moment of pain and the closure that comes.

The beauty concerning time is that it always moves forward, lessening the distance to the peace that was stolen away.

Every step forward you take on this road is a victory.

## TOGETHERNESS

I like to think about seeds and how they end up where they please, growing into wildflowers with their vibrant colors and free spirits. I like to think about the trees in the distance and the grass that dances in the wind like soft ocean waves. I like to think about how we are just as much a part of it all.

## *LETTING GO*

Serenity can only exist in our heads when we let go of the hate we have towards ourselves.

We tend to overwhelm our brains with expectations we simply can't attain.

Letting go, although difficult, is the seed that will grow into the serenity we deserve.

## THE BOOKS AT A GARAGE SALE

We are like books,
torn and tattered.

With stories unfinished,
our ending awaits.

But like books, all that matters
is the chapters and verses and the words they say.

## *WORDS WRITTEN ON THE BEACH*

The hateful words spoken into the sand of your heart will be washed away by waves of love and grace.

## OVERFLOW

It's okay to rest
and take care of the heart in your own chest.

We must first care for ourselves
before we can care for others.

So open your ribs and dig,
until you find the beating heart you forgot was there.

*Loving yourself is not selfish.*

When you do,
happiness fills your bones until it overflows,
touching everyone around you.

## *A WILDFLOWER, ALONE*

When you feel invisible, remember that the wildflower that blooms deep in the field, unseen and shyly swaying in the wind, is beautiful.

## THE EBB AND FLOW OF FRIENDSHIP

Everyone leaves when you need them to stay.
Everyone stays when you need them to leave.
Loving yourself is the consistency you seek,
since the only constant that exists is *you*.

## *LET IT BE*

Healing will come when we stop picking at our wounds
with shame and guilt.

## THE SUN SPEAKS WITH LOVE

Looming self-doubt clouds the sunrise we are gifted with
every single morning.

We tend to forget it's there,
as if we think we don't deserve it.

But, you can only take in the sunrise
if you open your eyes long enough to let your mind
imprint the picture on your heart.

Still, the sun comes alive hoping to remind you
you are worthy of its everlasting warmth.

So open your eyes, even if you're scared, and take it in
one color at a time.

## THE MOON BEHIND THE CLOUDS

Even when the clouds shield our eyes from the stars,
they still shine on.

Even when our negative thoughts hide our hearts
from the loveliness that we hold,
we still emanate beauty.

*Even when we can't see the light,
it is always there waiting.*

## WHATEVER YOU NEED TO BE

You are a red flower in the midst of yellow ones. Or a yellow flower in the midst of red ones. Or a rogue sunflower alone in a field. Or a dandelion dancing in someone's backyard. Never forget, you are uniquely and wonderfully made.

## SHEDDING SHAME

Shame is the most crushing of emotions
that bury us at such a young age.

We spend the rest of our lives digging ourselves
out of this pit.

What would this world look like if we taught our children
to esteem themselves?

Oh, how it would be glorious.

## THE SOUL, AN ATLAS

I unraveled my veins and found a map so intricate.

The center of it all is a heart so delicate.

Every heartbeat is a journey so incredibly elaborate.

Don't you see?

Every single one of us has a world inside ourselves worthy of our attention and love.

## THE COLORS ON A CANVAS

To be vulnerable is to pry open our ribs and show the scars on our hearts, all while they still beat.

Despite the scars, our hearts still sing.

To be vulnerable is to show this world there is such a thing as victory over pain.

## AN ATTEMPT TO REWRITE HISTORY

Somewhere between our first breaths and now, we learned how to hate ourselves.

I've been retracing my steps trying to find the origin of such a travesty.

## OVERWHELMED

You feel so small compared to the world. Yet, you are seen as infinitely valuable in the eyes of the ones around you. Never forget, when you see this vast existence and become overwhelmed, all I see is you and the vastness of everything about you that is lovely. I hope, one day, you can see what I see.

## WHILE EATING AN APPLE

The bruised fruit from our tired labors, although imperfect,
still tastes sweet.

## THE SMELL AFTER IT RAINS

I fell asleep to the sound of raindrops on the windows. The soft tapping brought me peace.

I awoke to find a pleasant scent waiting at my doorstep, an aroma that greeted me lovingly.

I am reminded that inside of all of us is a strength like a storm and a gentleness like petrichor.

## MORNING BREATHING EXERCISES

Breathe in the beauty that you see
when you look in the mirror.

Breathe out the lies this world has told you
about how one should look.

## THE SWEET SOUND OF HARMONY

I've been writing poems about the things I fear most to get
them off my chest so I can burn the pages and watch the
flames swallow up the pain before I rewrite the story.

I learned that if we embrace the mistakes we make they
become a canvas easily painted over with vibrant colors
in a way that tells a story of grace.

You see, *we're all in this together.*

Our beating hearts should be enough common ground to
love your neighbor and engage in community. So let's sing
along with life's melody feeling free to sing differently, our
voices blending into harmony.

As we grow, we realize a new perspective:
we're called to leave this place better than we found it.

We'll pick up the pieces and cherish them because it's where
we came from.

You know, it's the story behind the scars that shapes us, not
the pain we felt when they were made that allows us to keep
breathing, and stay afloat in the stormy waters that we go
through some days.

And when we see our brothers and sisters sinking, no matter how heavy the anchor, we'll reach for their hands until we've got them in our grasp and never let go.

And when we pull them to the shore, we will sing, and dance, and breathe in the sweet air we've been longing for.

*We're all in this together.*

# *WATER*

We hold a handful of seeds that we can only water by letting our well spill over.

## ONE WITH THE WALLS

If these walls could talk, they would ask if I was okay.

They would say,

*"I know your pain, but you're not alone. There are four of us, we'll be your home. Come inside and rest your head. Everything will be okay. I promise."*

## BITS AND FRAGMENTS

We are all just bits and fragments of the world around us.
However, it's the combination of those pieces and the way
they are arranged that makes us the unique pieces of art that
we all are. I've just very recently realized this. I used to tell
myself I was just a reflection of my surroundings and that
nothing about me was unique. Realizing that falsehood was
liberating. What would this world look like if we worked to
liberate the ones around us from negative self-talk? I think it
would look like a place that I'd be happy to call home.

## *I AM*

I am fragments of every wildflower I ever picked. Delicately,
I pull at the petals until they pop off and I send them away
with the wind.

I'll live in the fields like the wildflowers do, to find freedom
from the sadness this world spills like a wildfire from Earth's
open wound.

I am the buffalo that is born in my heart. Every heartbeat in
my chest is its hooves pounding on the pasture of my soul.
It runs gracefully through my veins, so wild and so free.

And even if you try, you cannot tame the beast. You can only
join in with its beauty, and together become a stampede of
passion and peace.

I am the stardust that is found in my bones. There is a galaxy
that exists in all of us, didn't you know?

And don't you see the light we all carry?

I know this world can be scary. But the stars and the moon
have a way to pierce the darkness softly.

I am me. You are you. We are us.
A collective beauty that sings in unison.

*Open your heart to the noise.*

## *ALONE IN MY CAR AT THE GROCERY STORE*

A shopping cart in the parking lot, empty besides a
crumpled receipt, holds a potential, holds a purpose, just as
we all do, even if we don't feel it at this moment.

## THROWING OURSELVES INTO THE OCEAN

The ocean waves take broken glass and smooth the edges, placing the pieces on the shore to remind us all we can make beauty out of the broken parts of who we are.

## A TREE FALLS, A SOUND IS MADE

I want to live in the forest so that every broken branch is heard as it tumbles to this earth. I want to understand the pain. I want to mend the branches to help restore those who have fallen. I want you to understand that despite the loneliness that lives in your head, I can hear the crack of breaking wood. And if you fall, I'll do my best to catch you.

## THE WEAVER AND THE LOOM

The world is a tapestry, the thread is our heartstrings. As long as we keep creating, keep living, keep breathing, we'll weave beauty into everything we touch with loving hands and passionate hearts.

## MY CHEST, A BLANK CANVAS

We are paintings, unfinished, longing to be touched with thick brushstrokes filling in the white spaces with vibrant, meaningful colors.

## A WALK DURING SPRING

You are a flower, so bloom.

You are a songbird, so sing.

You are a branch, so sway.

You are a river, so flow.

You are a light, so shine.

You are you, so be you.

## THE LEADED WINDOWS IN OUR DINING ROOM

The windows

*plea beg yearn*

for a moment of your time.

If you just look past the curtains,
you will see a world of beauty.

## BLOSSOM

We pluck the petals from the flowers that grow from our fingertips, because we are scared to show this world our truest colors. But nothing is more beautiful than the bouquet you hold in your hand, so let your flowers bloom.

## A WELCOME HELLO

Our eyes blink, tired and heavy, as the morning air tickles our cheeks, reminding us that the earth did not forget about us while we were asleep.

## THINGS TO DO ON A SPRING DAY

Smell the flowers. Feel the sun's power. Run barefoot in the grass. Touch the water's glistening surface with your fingertips. Grow in your heart, like the trees. Give yourself room to breathe and be free.

## SMALL-TOWN KID IN THE CITY

Another night, and I can't sleep.

I'm dreading work in the morning.

I take a walk down 15th Street to clear my head,
take some time to think.

I think I'll find out who I am, but all I find is an empty beer
can that reminds me of nights with old friends, trading
heartbeats for a cheap fix.

I wander past Victorian houses where people have found
a place to rest their bodies, and wonder why I'm not home
doing the same.

I remember growing up in a small town—misunderstood.

I moved to the city to find myself, but I got lost
in the shadows.

I cared too much about what others thought.

As I near the end of my walk, now on Summit Avenue,
I realize all that matters is our perspective of ourselves.

I wander home, tired, but at peace.

## WHAT YOU DON'T SEE

Today, you made someone smile, even if you didn't see it.

You brought joy to someone, even if you didn't know it.

You felt pain, but you surely overcame it.

You are the definition of strength, and this world
is better for it.

So, today, I thank you for who you are, even if you don't
think you deserve it.

## WHAT WE THINK ABOUT AT WORK

Our daydreams turn into reality when our passion meets action and the understanding that we were meant for so much more than just paying bills.

## WHAT LIES BENEATH

I was awakened in the middle of the night by a forest fire in my chest. There were old parts of me that were burning, but I was scared to let go of them. The moon whispered, "*Breathe.*" Smoke billowed from my mouth. I coughed up ashes and swallowed a waterfall to put out the flames. I fell into a deep sleep and awoke with the first signs of green sprouting from my heart. Sometimes, there are parts of us that need to die before we can truly grow. Sometimes, it takes a secondary succession to truly see the beauty that can arise from the scorched surface.

## THE FLUID NATURE OF EXISTENCE

When we sit for too long, we feel stagnant.

When we stand for too long, we feel the need to sit.

There is a unique flow to the way we exist, where we feel the need to move and be still, all in the same breath.

I promise you, there is a *calming in-between.*

## A FEATHER FOUND IN MY BACKYARD

A sparrow's feather falls from the sky and twirls to the earth like a maple seed.

The bird is no longer in sight, for its loss did not halt the movement of its strong wings.

Although we may lose a feather, let it not hinder our flight.

## WISDOM FROM GRANDPA'S GARDEN

Let us remove the roots of the weeds that grow in our hearts as a practice of self-care, for they suffocate our souls' ability to grow.

## FINDING PEACE

Let the sunset put to rest the worry in our heads
that keeps us up at night.

Let the sunrise awaken the goodness that exists in our bones
despite the circumstances we can't control.

## PERSEVERANCE

When our hearts break into pieces, we forever chase the feeling of them being whole again.

We desperately search for the fragments in the people we love and the places we go.

But the truth is, every single piece has stayed within us, so we carry everything we need to once again be complete.

## THE GOOD OL' DAYS

When everything good comes to an end, we reminisce about how it all began.

Why can't we have this same sense of joy as we live in the moment?

Live to understand the joy now, not yearn to go back to it.

*The past is not our home.*

## NATURE'S BECKONING

I cannot remember the last time I walked in the grass with bare feet to feel oneness with its roots. I cannot remember the last time I touched the running water of a small creek just to feel its pulse. I cannot remember the last time I saw a quiet flower without kidnapping it in a photograph.

The world around me is fearlessly living while I am too busy worrying about how I am slowly dying.

## BECOMING ONE WITH THE MOTION

The wind can never be tamed, just like the world around us that causes us to sway back and forth.

We're always moving; even when we're still, our chests continue to rise and fall.

The breeze can never be domesticated.

So, be a feather and let the movement be a dance for this gift of existence we hold in our hands.

## WHAT WE ARE GIVEN

You gaze softly through the fence.

Is it a yearning for the other side?

Or do you sympathize with those who will never find
contentment with the green grass that lies
beneath their feet?

## A WALK TO THE RAIL YARD

I went for a walk with my camera to find a bit of inspiration
the wall behind my desk wasn't providing.

I decided to head towards the rail yard to find some graffiti
on the railcars.

As I walked up 8th Street, I was approached by a tall man
who seemed to be homeless.

He asked, very timidly, if I could take a picture of him
and his friends.

He said they'd never been able to take a photo together, and
he'd always wanted one.

He didn't want money, or a ride, or directions
to the nearest shelter.

He simply wanted a moment captured so he could
remember this time with his friends.

My heart broke and I agreed.

*Click.*

I showed them their beautiful faces.

They laughed and smiled at the image, which brought me
such joy. I asked where I could send a copy.

They looked at each other, then back at me.

Their eyes hit me like a railcar going full speed.

One replied,

*"Well, I have a friend whose house I sometimes stay at, but I don't know what his address is."*

The weight of the reality that hung in this moment
reminded me of just how privileged I am
to have pictures with my friends,
to have a place to rest my head.

I couldn't help but wonder where they slept that night
as I crawled into my comfy bed.

## DISMANTLE, RESTORE

Let's wage war on what breaks people,
not broken people, themselves.

Let us rebuild *together*.

## TO GRIEVE IS TO GROW

The trees shed their leaves with the understanding that
their branches will be filled, once again, in a season
not so far away.

# GROWTH

As our stems sprout, we can offer what we've learned about
what it means to grow to the ones around us.

## SOFT SKIN

There's beauty in the brokenness of the soft skin
that hides our hearts from the pain that wants in.

We live in a world that's crumbling, where self-inflicted pain
hurts less than what we feel in our brains.

We're a generation told to build our own homes,
without solid ground or the right materials.

We fight fire with fire, let hate swallow our souls' desire,
while the pain in our hearts becomes dire.

Despite this, there's a beauty in the brokenness of the soft
skin we will wear proudly as our armor,
with love as our weapon,
as we tell this world *we won't give in.*

## A LETTER TO GROW

*Dear bitter heart,*

I think it's time you move out. I put your clothes in a bag on the porch. I'm sorry if it rains, but maybe then the water will wash clean everything we said and didn't mean.

Sincerely,

*me*

## *THE WAY IN WHICH WE HEAL*

Your head will mend despite the voices that haunt you.

Your heart will mend despite the people that broke you.

Your eyes will mend despite the pain you saw around you.

Your soul will mend despite the evil that surrounds you.

*You will mend.*

*lovelyseeds* - 93

## OXYGEN

Reflect and step back. What in this world gives you breath?
I find oxygen in conversations that help people grow. I find
oxygen in art where one's honest creativity is shown. I find
oxygen in people who strive to leave this place better than
they found it.

## DRIVING HOME FROM THE HOSPITAL

The images in our rearview mirror grow smaller
the farther we get away.

Every breath we take is a step away from the pain
that so desperately tries to strangle us.

The enemy of pain is perseverance,
is the distance that grows between our selves,
and the moment of hurt.

## THE HOUSE WE GREW UP IN

For some, the house where we grew up was a vessel full of loving memories.

For others, it was a vessel that was broken, where love leaked through the cracks in the drywall.

For some, the four walls and roof were a sacred place we never wanted to leave.

For others, it was a jail cell they couldn't wait to escape and be free.

This dichotomy is important to understand when we seek to heal the brokenness of others, because the house we grew up in is the origin of everything we know about love.

## US, THE ARCHITECTS OF OUR OWN REBUILDING

The vase falls in slow motion from its shelf.

It is in the moment between the fall and the ground that time stands still.

It is the last moment we are whole before we are shattered.

It is in that moment the blueprint is made that we'll use to reassemble ourselves back into wholeness, once again.

## PURE UNADULTERATED JOY

When we deconstruct existence down to its bare bones,
aren't we left with just a feeling? I used to think I needed
to work towards something I could hold in my hands,
something I could put in my pocket. But the flowers I picked
always died. The photographs I took always faded. My
friends came and went like this moody Midwest weather. I
realized what I was trying to hold onto was so temporary.
I realized all that is left after a house fire is the memories
created within. I realized life is all about how we feel. There
is a pure joy that comes when we choose to be present. There
is a happiness that leaks into our bones.

## *LOVELY*

We're all made up of scarred skin and fragile bones that
crack slowly under the weight of racism and hate.

We all have a chest that is home to a broken heart that beats
to the drums of perseverance because we live in a world that
passes judgments on appearance.

If you've ever been bullied, beat up, or brought down I want
you to hear this:

*You are lovely. Your heart is lovely. Your body is lovely. Your soul
is lovely.*

I wish I could apologize for the sins of a thousand men
and take away the pain caused by all of them.

I know I'm not perfect, but hear me out.
The voices of hate are screaming loud.
But I hear whispers of love in the crowd.

*Can you hear it now?*

If you don't, I know you're just confused.
Maybe it was the way you were raised.
Maybe you just wanted something to blame.

I have a hard time understanding the way you think but
here's some truth:

*You can be lovely, too.*

You can treat others like you want to be treated.

Maybe your kindergarten teacher forgot to mention that,
just like our history books forgot to mention
all the imperfections.

We were taught nationalism, not real life lessons.

So at least understand this:

Everything you read, see, or hear isn't all there is to know
to create a predefined understanding of a race, culture, or
religion.

Not even the words I'm saying now, but listen.

If I prick my finger, and you prick yours the same color of
blood will drip on the floor.

We're all just scarred skin and fragile bones trying to make
the best of this world, our home.

So choose to be lovely because the choice is our own.

## THE MYTH OF FINDING BALANCE

I was told there was a balance to this life as if there was a
way to control our existence and everything that happens in
it. I can tell you for certain, this is untrue. There is only the
wind and the ocean. Sometimes we are the waves, viciously
crashing on the shoreline at the mercy of the wind and
where it wants to take us. Other times we are the wind, in
control of how and where we move the ocean. Life is about
finding a sense of peace in it all.

## MY BECOMING

I am a waterfall.

I was made to spill over, to overflow out of my bones the parts of me that belong to this world.

What I've learned is that, although I am thankful for the deer that comes to take a drink, I was made simply to be me.

So, I will continue to spill over, to overflow,
to embrace who I am.

## *DOE*

I went for a walk in a wooded area to clear my head. I came across the sound of movement.

There were rustling leaves and branches. I had an overwhelming feeling that I wasn't alone.

I positioned my head slightly to the side to get a better look ahead.

I locked eyes with a beautiful doe. We stood there for just a moment and bathed in curious wonderment, a moment I wish I could carry in my pocket.

Our gaze was broken by the hands of fear. I took a step back, cracking a twig with my heel.

The doe fled as though the sound was a gunshot.

Do you feel, at times, we let fright suffocate moments of wonderment we should revel in for a little while longer?

Wouldn't this world be better off if patience and compassion spilled from our bones, helping us grow towards a better understanding?

We fear what we don't know.

When we get to know, progress flows.

## SHEDDING TOXICITY: A HOW-TO

When you figure out who the toxic people in your life
are, set yourself on fire and walk slowly back across the
bridge that brought you to them, making sure every single
footboard is set ablaze before you reach the other side.

## WHERE WAX MEETS FLAME

Let's put candles in our chests to illuminate our hearts,
so that we can remember what this world looked like before
it got so dark.

## THE BEAUTY THAT FLOWS FROM EMPOWERMENT

At an early age, you were told to keep your mouth shut.

All those years of words dancing behind your teeth are
about to spill across the floor and create
the most beautiful ballet.

The sway, the movement, the music that plays,
captures hearts as you tell your story.

## *SHIFTING THE WAY WE THINK*

You see darkness. I see a candle waiting to be lit.

It's all about *perspective*.

## WE ARE RICH WITH PLENTY

Gold drips from the petals of flowers.

Diamonds can be found swimming in the ocean.

Poetry falls from trees in the autumn.

Timeless hymns can be heard from songbirds in the spring.

What else could anyone want or need?

## A PAST FULL OF DEAD HOUSEPLANTS

Don't plant a garden if you don't intend on watering it,
for nothing grows from empty promises.

## A BREEZE

Be air to the lungs that suffocate under the weight
of self-doubt.

## A SPRING SHOWER

Be water for the seeds of self-love that rest in the hearts of the ones who exist around you.

## *LESSONS LEARNED IN HINDSIGHT*

Progress is to learn, to grow, to be okay with the mistakes.

It was my skinned knees and battered heart that brought me to this place of truly living.

## GENERATIONAL GROWTH

Sticks and stones break our bones.

Hateful words plague generations of souls.

Don't let your words be the heavy yoke your children give to their children.

## WHERE WE FIND PROGRESSION

Sometimes you're the teacher, and sometimes
you're the student.

Our entire existence consists of teaching and learning.

When this comes to a halt, we need to reevaluate where our
priorities are.

Progress can only come with newfound understandings.

Let's open our ears to hear the sound of experiences that are
different than our own.

*This is where we grow.*

## WISDOM FROM GRANDPA

Be *gentle*.

Be *fierce*.

Be whatever it is you need to be to make this world better than the way you found it.

# *BLOOM*

When our petals begin to show, our valiant colors give hope
to those who need it most.

## THE GARDEN BENEATH OUR RIBS

If words are seeds, let flowers grow from your mouth,
not weeds.

If our hearts are gardens, plant those flowers in the chests of
the ones who are growing around you.

## RESTORING FAITH IN THE HUMAN RACE

There is a beauty in the stillness that surrounds
our fragile skin.

We just need to take the time to open our eyes.

We just need to take the time to realize not everything
in this world is terrible.

## SOMETHING FOR ALL OF US

There is a place for you in the chaos and the calm, a place
for you in love and in heartbreak, a place for you among
the tallest buildings and the smallest trees. There is a place
for you and a place for me. There is a place where we can
coexist in unity with sweet harmony. There is always a place.

## THIS CITY IS A MUSEUM

There is art all around.

I see it as I walk up and down the streets.

It's in our bones.

It's the scars on our skin that hide underneath our clothes.

It's our beating hearts that paint our insides red.

This city is a museum, and we are the masterpieces within.

## BEAUTY IN THE BONES

I saw beauty buried inside the bones of a broken man whose
home is the same city streets we are told never to walk alone
after the sun has set.

His bloodshot eyes, red like a fresh wound, told the story of
all the trials he had ever endured.

As I walked past, selfishly hoping he wouldn't ask for some
change, he smiled.

I could see the weight of his pain trying to pull down
on each side of his face.

But still he held his smile in place,
igniting my lips to do the same.

This man, with alcohol in his veins, dirty clothes on his
skin, and a heart full of burdens, still knew how to be kind,
despite my selfish heart.

There is a beauty buried, yes.

But our eyes can be shovels, ready to dig for gold inside the
bones of the ones around us.

## THE WARMTH THAT COMES FROM BURNING

You are a wildfire, a fiery soul, a burning passion, a smoldering coal.

You have the means to set ablaze the hearts whose fire had burned out before they found you.

You are the match that lights the candle this dark world so desperately needs.

## THE AROMA OF A FLOWER SHOP

The beauty in a whole bouquet of flowers lies within the multitude of colors and the array of sizes and shapes of the stems and petals.

So similarly, does the diversity of people lend beauty to the whole of humanity.

## FOOD STAMPS

I heard a news story about a woman who sold her food
stamps to buy cigarettes and cocaine.

Everyone wondered how somebody could be so selfish with
the taxpayer's dollar.

But I want to understand, I want to see how she could
become so broken.

The news doesn't talk about her fatherless childhood, or
her drugged-out mom, or the barbaric boys who beat her
because she tried to say no to the way they wanted
to use her body.

I wish the hands of empathy could replace
the spaces between her fingers holding cigarettes,
and mercy's heart could beat in her chest until
healing pumps through her veins, replacing the cocaine.

I want the world to see that there is so much more to every
single one of us underneath the pain.

## WATCHING THE NEWS

When this world is thirsty, let your words be water.

When this world is hungry, let your words be bread.

When this world is dark, let your words be light.

We all have a voice, so let it speak love.

## *LENDING A HAND*

The weight of existence is too heavy for one to carry.

When your heart beats for others, you feel their happiness and their pain, their love and their hate.

It can be exhausting, but we cannot pick ourselves up when our hands are already full.

Let us, instead, hold each other up.

## OUR WORDS

Speak only if your words are intended for positive growth.

At times, your voice will be fierce.

Other times, it will be soft.

Equally as important, you will be silent as you give others the space to talk.

Speak only if your words will build humanity instead of tearing it down.

## GOING ON A WALK

I find words written in the eyes of passersby. I collect them
as I wander the sidewalks and arrange the pieces into poetry.
If only I could give back to these strangers what they have
given me, a reminder that we all are beautiful,
despite the state of the times.

## SPEAK LOVE

Speak words into hearts you wish were spoken into yours.

## WHAT THE NEWS DOESN'T TEACH US

In this broken world, we must tear down the systems and circumstances that break us, not simply tear down our selves.

## WHAT IT MEANS TO SET A GOOD EXAMPLE

Let's write stories with our actions that will leave footprints towards a better place for future souls.

Let's tear up the blueprints for broken homes,
and teach our children how to learn and grow
in a future full of positive progression.

Let us teach that mistakes can turn into learned lessons in a blanket of forgiveness, instead of negative aggression.

## PRACTICING EMPATHY

My empathy towards a fellow human does not justify their negative actions.

Rather, it is an admission that we are, in fact, simply human.

To progress, we must address the root of evil, not just its bitter fruit.

## LISTEN

We long to lose ourselves in the lost art of listening.

When you hear someone talk, listen to their heart until you can feel their heart beat in your chest.

As we open our ears and lean in, we learn ways to love those who have experiences that look different than ours.

## OUR HANDS

Our hands are meant to hold gently, caress softly, and embrace lovingly.

Our hands are not meant to lift lifeless bodies from the wreckage of another bomb that never should have fallen from the same sky we look to for protection.

We're meant for so much more than the sadness that spills from our televisions.

## IDENTITY: A STORY OF SHATTERED GLASS

Our identity is like a glass vase.

*Fragile, unique, and beautiful.*

The moment it is knocked onto the floor, it cracks and becomes difficult to put back together.

Compassion is helping find the shards and piece them back together with love and understanding.

If we do not show compassion to the ones around us who are shattered, we mustn't be shocked by the cuts we receive from the sharp edges of their brokenness.

## TOGETHER, A STRONGER PRESENCE

We yearn to reunite our hearts, uprooted by vicious winds, with the fertile soil that allows us to grow.

As our hearts dig in, our veins intertwine with others with the hope that the wind will not have a chance to uproot our selves ever again.

## THE THINGS WE TEACH

When we say,

*"Boys will be boys,"*

We teach our daughters that love can look like bruises.

We teach our sons that women's bodies can be battlegrounds where they deal with their insecurities.

Let us raise our children to respect one another, and set a new standard for future generations.

## SUFFERING

Children see the pain in their parents' eyes.

Their mother holds them close, tells them it'll be all right.

Tells them they'll find a better life.

And the father doesn't know, but they hear him cry at night.

Every day is a fight to survive.

Children are suffering,
simply because of the place they were born.

And even if they get out, they'll be exposed to judgement
because of the color of their skin.

Can we, for a second, talk about people, not politics?

Can we address humanity, not policy?

Because CHILDREN are suffering, simply because they were
a seed planted deep in the womb of a refugee.

This world is not black and white, so let's stop polarizing
and forming sides.

Because we all have a heartbeat, we all were a seed buried
deep in the womb of a woman, just some of us were born in
a war-torn country.

Some of us were born into a family without the understanding that just because our father and mother were of a certain race or religion, we'd be treated differently.

Can we, for a second, at least acknowledge that this existence is so much more complicated than a piece of paper with a signature?

Now, I don't have the answers.

I don't know how to fix things.

I just want to let the world know, that there is beauty in loving humanity.

There is beauty in trying to understand that every woman, child, and man was once a seed buried deep in the womb of a woman.

And when we all took our first breath, we deserved, at least, a fighting chance.

No matter our religion.
No matter the color of our skin.
No matter our country of origin.

## OCEAN WAVE

We can be powerful or gentle, peaceful or wild.

Either way, we are inspiring and revolutionary.

We will be whatever it is we need to be.

We will move you if you let us, or crash into you if you get in our way.

We are an ocean wave.

# *RESTORE*

Our leaves wilt and fall to the ground.

## THE COOLING OF WAX

A candle flickers and eventually fades,
just like the pain we endure throughout our days
on this wild and beautiful earth.

## A DEATHBED WITHOUT REGRETS

Do not wait until your hair turns gray, like the clouds on a melancholic rainy day, to realize that playing it safe never stopped your bones from growing fragile.

So dance until your feet are sore, sing until your voice grows hoarse, and laugh like you did as a child before this world broke you.

## ENJOY NOW, ENJOY TOMORROW

I extend my hand and receive this gift from the sky.

The snowflakes kiss my palm and quickly disappear.

I am reminded that everything will eventually melt away.

Our lives are merely the time between our initial descent,
like these snowflakes, and the final destination.

To be present is to cherish
this breath, this life, this humanity.

Let us enjoy the chill, for now, then bury our regrets in the
snow and watch them melt away when the songbirds sing.

## GARDENING WITH GRANDPA

When I was young, I never understood why my grandpa would plant flowers in the spring, just to watch them suffocate under the weight of winter's white. As I reflect, I now see that despite the cold, he understood that there is beauty in this one finite life we hold. I am reminded of our finiteness every time the snow slowly dances to the ground. I am reminded of our finiteness every time the soil births flowers in the springtime.

# WHAT TRANSCENDS THE GRAVE

Our bones will wither away,
but the love that we spill will stay.

## WITHERING

Petals wilt in the sun, like our skin,
as we grow old, tired, and cold.

There is a beauty in our aging bodies,
just as in wilting flowers.

## ANOTHER DAY IN HOSPICE

The slowing of your heartbeat makes my heart race.

Death is a part of life, but as you close your eyes and say goodbye, I can't help but stare at you and cry.

Oh, could my heart beat for you and my eyes see for you.

## *SAY WHAT YOU NEED TO SAY*

I wish we didn't wait to say how we feel to the ones we love the most until all that's left of them is their ghost.

## A RAINY DRIVE TO WORK

When it rains, I think of you. As the raindrops touch my skin, I'm at peace, knowing they came from where you are.

## FLOWERS AND HEADSTONES

We plant flowers in cemeteries out of mourning. We see their growth as something beautiful, just like the beauty found in healing. The sadness never completely goes away, but the flowers in our hearts outgrow the pain. *This is progress.*

## AIR BETWEEN OUR FINGERS

Life is the air between our fingers. It is always there, but only sometimes do we feel it. It is the air between our fingers when we learned how to crawl on the floor of our parents' house they worked themselves to the bone for. Life is the air between our fingers as we ride our bikes for the first time, and it's the air between our fingers when we fall off and skin our knuckles. Life is the air between our fingers when we find out what it's like to hold hands with another and it's the air between our fingers when we hold a newborn child. Life is the air between our fingers as we work ourselves to the bone to provide loved ones a place to call home. It is the air between our fingers that develop arthritis as we age, like a wilting flower that still holds its beauty.

Life is the air between our fingers as they grow weak to the point they can no longer give you what you need from them.

It is in this moment that I want you to know, you've given everything you must to this world and the ones you love, so you have nothing left to prove or show. Give your hands rest, and let the air between your fingers kiss them softly goodnight.

## *LOVELY SEEDS*

The peaceful places in our heads we yearn to exist in are where we find the seeds of our becoming.

Let us plant them in a garden where they can grow into whatever it is they are meant to be.

First, we must find the most fertile soil and lose ourselves in all the love it has to offer.

We bury ourselves deep.

Here we hold a handful of seeds that only we can water on our own, so we'll spill over and give ourselves what we need.

As our stems sprout, we can offer what we've learned about what it means to grow to the ones around us.

And when our petals begin to show, our valiant colors give hope to those who need it most.

Eventually, our leaves wilt and fall to the ground.

Here, they become one with the soil.

This is not an end, rather, it is a chance for

*rebirth.*

## ACKNOWLEDGEMENTS

I'd like to dedicate this book to my grandmother who raised me to be a light in this dark world and my grandfather who taught me to "leave a place better than you found it." It is my hope that this book does just that.

A special thanks to my wife, Loni Swaney, for being the biggest inspiration in my life and always reminding me that there is value in the words I write and share with the world.

Additional thanks go out to Amanda Lovelace, Cyrus Parker, Trista Mateer, William Bortz, Iain Thomas, Morgan Nikola-Wren, Alicia Cook, Josh Gilbert, Hillary McBride, Kyle Fasel, the Swaney and McComber families, and finally Michelle Halket from Central Avenue Publishing, who is the very reason this book was able to get into your hands.

The spoken word versions of the following poems can be found on Spotify, iTunes, and Apple Music under the artist name, R. H. Swaney:

Weather Talk; The Voices In Our Heads; Freedom; The Sweet Sound Of Harmony; I Am; Small Town Kid In The City; What Lies Beneath; A Walk To The Rail Yard; Soft Skin; Pure Adulterated Joy; Lovely; Doe; Beauty In The Bones; Food Stamps; Suffering; Air Between Our Fingers; Lovely Seeds.